NELSON

TOR FREEMAN
AND
JUDE FREEMAN

WALKER
BOOKS

For Maureen and the whole Nqayana family,
with our love
J.F. & T.F.

First published 2009 by Walker Books Ltd
87 Vauxhall Walk, London SE11 5HJ

4 6 8 10 9 7 5 3

Text © 2009 Tor Freeman and Judith Freeman
Illustrations © 2009 Tor Freeman

This book has been typeset in Bembo Educational
and Myriad Sketch

Printed and bound in China

British Library Cataloguing in Publication Data:
a catalogue record for this book is available from the British Library

ISBN: 978-1-4063-1823-4

www.walker.co.uk

Glossary of South African words

ouma [o-mah]: grandmother (Afrikaans)

oupa [o-pah]: grandfather (Afrikaans)

mealie [mee-lee]: an ear of corn, corn on the cob

bakkie [buk-ky]: a small pick-up truck (Afrikaans)

A Long Journey

Flora and Annie lived with their mother in a big city called Cape Town. Today was the start of the school holidays, and the sisters were excited because they were going to visit their grandparents. Ouma and Oupa lived three hundred miles away in the country, so Flora and Annie would have to travel on a bus.

Flora and Annie often went to stay with Ouma and Oupa in the school holidays, because Ma worked and couldn't look after them. But this would be their first journey on their own.

Before they left, Flora and Annie
helped to make their favourite
sandwiches, and Ma slipped
some sweets and
fizzy drinks
into their
lunchboxes
as a treat.

9

At the busy terminal, Ma got onto
the bus with Flora and Annie to help
them choose their seats.

Flora said Annie could sit by the
window so that she could see out, and
Ma said she was proud of Flora for
being so kind.

10

Once they were settled, Ma put their packed lunches safely under their seats. She spoke to the bus driver and told him where Ouma and Oupa lived. Then she said, "Please take special care of my girls!"

"Don't worry," said the driver with a friendly smile. "I will guard them like a lion with two cubs!"

Ma gave Flora
and Annie extra big
hugs and a kiss
each and said,
"Now you be
good girls for
your ouma and oupa,
and I will come and see
you as soon as I can."

When the bus set
off, Flora and
Annie waved
and waved until
their mother
was just a speck
in the distance.

12

It felt a bit strange at first, being on their own on the bus, so the sisters sat quietly, holding hands and looking out of the window. But there was so much to see that they soon forgot Ma wasn't with them and started to enjoy the journey.

They opened their packed lunches and decided to eat their sweets right away!

The bus sped through the busy city, past tall buildings and through rushing traffic.

It went down quiet streets with big houses and leafy gardens.

Then the bus came to the townships on the edge of the city. It drove past hundreds of small houses built very close together, like little coloured boxes.

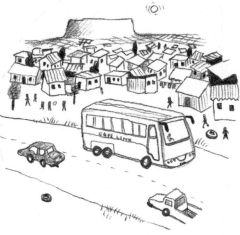

Flora and Annie saw people everywhere – walking, playing, selling, dancing and cooking.

They even saw a man having his hair cut outside a barber's shop!

15

Now they were in the country,
the city far behind. Here there were
mountains and a few lonely farms.
Every now and then the bus went past
a farm stall.

Flora and Annie saw wooden carvings of bush animals like giraffes and elephants, and brightly coloured fabrics that waved to them as the bus rushed by.

Soon Annie's
head began to
nod and she fell
asleep leaning on
Flora's shoulder.

Flora felt very
grown up. A few
weeks ago Ma had
said to her, "You know
that I have to work in the
school holidays.

Do you think
you are old
enough now to
go on the bus
without me?

18

"Ouma and Oupa would meet you at the bus stop, but it would be your job to look after your little sister until then."

Flora had thought for a bit and then said, "Yes, Ma, I can do that."

"I'm sure you can," her mother had said. "And Flora," she had added, "are you still frightened of Nelson?"

Flora's heart had jumped when she'd heard Ma say that.

Nelson was Ouma's big red
rooster. He lived in his house
in the back garden with
all of his hens. He had a
proud tail, red and black
chest feathers and a loud
piercing crow.

He had mean
yellow eyes and
a pointed beak.
Nelson was the chief
rooster in the neighbourhood.
Flora hated him.

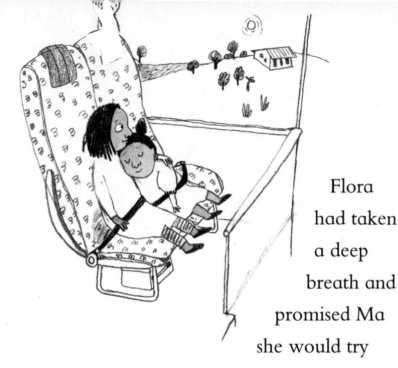

Flora
had taken
a deep
breath and
promised Ma
she would try
hard not to be frightened – after all,
she *was* old enough to look after Annie
on the bus!

As Flora gazed out of the bus
window, she saw that the sun was
sinking lower in the sky. She began to
see things and places she recognized.

22

"Wake up, Annie! I can see the sea!"
Annie opened her eyes and looked
sleepily around. "And I can see Ouma
and Oupa!" she shouted.

Flora and Annie jumped off the bus
and straight into Ouma's arms while
Oupa went to get their bags. Ouma
smelled of baking, and sea and
sun, and the cream she used to
make her skin shiny and soft.
They knew now that their
journey was over and
their holiday was
about to
begin.

A Dropped Egg

Flora and Annie loved staying with
their grandparents. At home they only
had a small yard to play in, but Ouma
and Oupa had a big front garden. Their
house was in a small township where
most people knew each other, and Ouma
and Oupa knew *everyone*, so there was
always somebody to play with.

27

In the garden there were trees to climb, shrubs to hide behind and insects to discover. Oupa had made a swing by hanging an old tyre from a high branch, and Flora and Annie took turns trying to be the best swinger.

28

There was
an apple tree
to knock
apples from,
and they even

knew how to pick

prickly pears from

the prickly

pear bush

and eat them

without

getting

prickled.

29

Inside the house, Flora and Annie spent a lot of time with Ouma.

Their grandmother was a very good cook, and the kitchen was her favourite place. She cooked for the family, for her church and sometimes for other people in the township.

Ouma was always
busy with
something,
and there were
always delicious
smells to sniff
and little jobs to
be done.

There were so
many wonderful things about
staying with Ouma and
Oupa. But there
was also …

31

NELSON!

Ouma was very proud of her big red rooster. He followed her around when she was doing her outside jobs.

When she was in
the kitchen, Nelson
would often stick
his head through
the open window
to be fed.

33

Annie loved
it when Nelson
did this, and she
would feed him
handfuls of maize
from a sack on the floor.

Flora did *not* love it,
and she would hide
behind Ouma.

Annie had never been
frightened of Nelson.
She would skip
down the

garden path to the
gate and back
again all by herself.

34

She would
stroll round
the bushes on
her own.
She would even
feed the
hens outside when
Nelson was right there!
Annie was not afraid.
Flora would only go
into the back garden

by herself when
she knew
Nelson was
asleep in
his house.

One morning when Flora and Annie were playing on the tyre swing with their friends, Ouma called Flora into the kitchen. She had a little job for her.

"Flora," said Ouma, "I am baking a cake. Could you go to the henhouse and get me four eggs, please?"

The chicken coop was in the back garden, and Nelson's house was inside it.

"What about Nelson?" asked Flora.

"Nelson is sleeping," said Ouma.
"But even if he wakes up he won't
hurt you. You mustn't be frightened of
Nelson. You're a big girl now."

Flora knew she would have to go. Her grandmother was right: she *was* a big girl.

She *peeked* her head out of the back door.

Then she *ran* across the garden to the mimosa tree.

She *peered* round the trunk, very, very slowly. No sign of Nelson.

38

She *tiptoed* across
to the coop.

She opened
the hatch and
reached in.

Carefully she felt
around in the straw and
very gently lifted out four
smooth, warm eggs.

39

Using her T-shirt as a basket,
Flora *sped* back to the
mimosa tree.
She *peered* round
the trunk, very,
very slowly,
and came face
to face with ...
NELSON!

There he was,
staring at her
with his mean
yellow eyes! Flora
was so frightened
that she couldn't
move.

Nelson started to
squawk and flap his wings.
That made Flora move
all right!

She ran
as fast as she could
to the back door and
burst into the kitchen.

"Whatever is all this?" exclaimed Ouma.

Flora looked down at her T-shirt and realized she must have dropped one of the eggs when she ran away. She turned to the window.

Sure enough, an egg was lying smashed on the ground. Flora felt like crying.

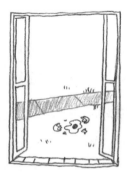

"For goodness' sake, Flora!" said Ouma. "Don't worry. Three eggs is enough to bake my cake."

For the rest of
the morning,
Flora and
Annie helped
Ouma in the
kitchen. When
the cake was baked,

Oupa came in for
a slice. Ouma told
Oupa what had
happened.
"Well, I
think this cake
is three-egg
delicious!"
said Oupa.

But Flora still felt sad. She couldn't stop thinking about Nelson. She wished she hadn't run away and dropped the egg. She wished she had been braver.

A Big Wave

It was a hot and sunny Saturday, and
in the evening Ma would be arriving
on the bus from Cape Town. Flora and
Annie couldn't wait to see her.

Oupa said, "While we're waiting,
shall we spend the day at the beach?"

"Yay!" cried Flora and Annie
together.

The girls helped their grandmother
prepare a picnic of mealies, sandwiches
and the leftover three-egg cake.
Ouma brought out her old shopping
bag, and they packed towels,
swimming costumes and their
favourite beach toys.

Everyone piled into Oupa's
bakkie, and off they set.

It was a perfect day.
Flora and Annie
had a wonderful
time. They
paddled in the
shallow water
and jumped
over the tiny

waves. They played

with their beach ball

and raced hermit

crabs against

each other.

Oupa helped them
build a mini
village out of
sticks and
shells and
dried leaves.

After lunch
their grandparents rested in the shade.

Oupa put his old cap
over his face to
keep out the sun.

After a while, the tide started to come
in, and the waves began to get bigger.
Oupa stretched. "One more swim
and then it's time to go home," he said.

He held Annie's hand
and together they walked
down into the sea.

The waves looked enormous.

Flora said, "Ouma, please can we stay here? I don't feel like swimming."

"Of course," said Ouma.

Flora and her grandmother watched Oupa and Annie splashing around. A big wave washed over Annie, and Flora felt worried.

But Oupa pulled Annie up out of the water and Flora could see that her sister was laughing.

"You know, Flora," said Ouma gently, "when I was a little girl, I was always too frightened to swim in the sea. I thought a big wave might come and wash me away."

"Really?" said Flora. She couldn't imagine Ouma being frightened of anything.

"Yes," smiled Ouma. "I would sit on my own on the beach and wish I could play with the others in the sea. Then, one day, do you know what I thought to myself?"

"What?"
asked Flora.

"Well," said Ouma, "I thought to myself, That big wave doesn't frighten me. That big wave is just a lot of water. It's the same as lightning, which is just a big light; and thunder, which is just a big noise. It's nothing to be frightened of."

Flora thought for a moment. "And a bit like a rooster is just a big chicken?"

Ouma laughed. "Exactly!"

On the way
home, Flora
was quiet. She
was thinking
about big waves,
and big chickens.

Back at the house,
Flora and Annie went straight to the
kitchen to help Ouma prepare
Ma's welcome supper.

The girls were in charge of washing and peeling the vegetables.

Ouma was making Ma's favourite stew, from when Ma was a little girl.

Suddenly Annie cried,
"Look! It's Nelson!"

Sure enough, there he
was, perched up on the
windowsill. Annie
scooped up
some maize.
She held her hand out flat
towards the rooster.
"Here, Nelson,"
she said.
Nelson pecked
at her hand
and Annie giggled.
"It tickles!" she
laughed.

Flora thought
it looked fun.
A rooster is just
a big chicken,
she thought.
And a big
chicken doesn't
frighten me! She scooped up her
own handful of maize from
the sack and went
to stand
beside
Annie.

Flora took
a deep breath
and brought up
her hand, very
slowly. Nelson
looked right
at her with his
beady yellow eyes.
Flora opened her hand,
nice and flat just as
Annie had done.
Quick as a flash,
Nelson pecked
some grain.

It didn't hurt! Just as Annie had said, it tickled! Flora laughed.

"You don't scare me, big chicken!" she said. And that made Annie and Ouma laugh too.

Suddenly they heard the noise of an engine starting up outside, and Oupa's voice calling, "Let's go, girls. It's time to collect your ma from the bus stop!"

Flora and Annie rushed outside to the bakkie. They couldn't wait to see their mother. They had so much to tell her, and Flora just knew that Ma was going to be very, very proud!